CHRISTMAS CHILLS

MAVIS SYBIL

Contents

Chapter 1

"Mmm mm mmm," said Jack.

"What?" I took out my earbuds so I could hear him.

"I said, Santa is kinda creepy."

I turned around in my seat to get a look at my little brother. He was gazing out the window through his thick glasses, watching the flat, snow-covered farmland between our house and the grocery store.

"That's random," I said.

"What do you mean?" asked Mom. She took one hand off the wheel of the car and reached for the radio to turn it down.

"I don't know. He just. He's spying on people all year long and then he breaks into everyone's homes and eats your cookies and stuff."

I had to correct him. My brother would not smear Santa's good name without an argument.

"He doesn't break into homes. He is invited into homes. And he doesn't steal any cookies. He only eats the cookies that we leave out for him."

Mom added, "It's like how we always leave a tip for the cleaning staff when we go to a hotel."

I nodded.

"You know who else only comes into your house if they're invited?" Jack asked.

"Who?" I replied.

"Vampires."

"Okay, Santa is not a vampire, Jack!" Mom said.

Jack added, "And he only comes out at night on Christmas eve."

Mom laughed.

I thought about it, too. "You know what? I think Jack has a point. Santa lives at the North Pole, right?"

"Yeah," said Mom, her voice a little bit guarded.

"Well, it's nighttime like half the year there. That would be a perfect place for a vampire to live."

"That's true!" Jack's eyes got big by the realization.

Mom sighed, "Okay, you two. Santa is not a vampire, okay? Vampires don't make toys and eat cookies. Hannah, please stop encouraging him."

"Maybe we should put out Halloween decorations for Christmas instead of Christmas decorations," I said.

"Yeah!" Jack was into it now. Halloween was his favorite holiday. "And we can make blood cookies for vampire Santa!"

I laughed. Mom had heard enough and she turned the music back up, which my brother and I both knew meant that the conversation was over.

Mom found a parking spot at the grocery store. The cold, crisp mid-December air felt like a smack in the face after getting out of the warm, cozy car. We walked across the muddy, slushy snow on the pavement, toward the jingle-jangle sound of a bell.

I elbowed my brother a bit and whispered, "Look out. Vampire up ahead."

I pointed to the man standing outside the entrance to the grocery store dressed as Santa, ringing a bell and asking customers to leave donations in his big red bucket. Jack laughed. But as we got closer, Jack's smile faded. When we were almost at the entrance, Santa stepped sideways, blocking our path.

"Would you be kind enough to donate to underprivileged children this holiday?" His teeth were yellow and a few of them were missing. His eyes were round and wide open. His pupils were tiny, like someone drew little black dots on a ping-pong ball. And he didn't blink as much as people should. He smelled like fish.

"I'm sorry. I. Uh. I don't have any cash," Mom forced a polite smile. I could see that Mom thought he was creepy, too, but she was always polite.

"That's fine," said Santa, "You can use a debit card during checkout to take out some cash."

"Um. Okay," said Mom, who looked nervous. She pulled us closer to her and walked with us around the creepy Santa, putting herself in between him, me and Jack. I looked behind us as we went in; Santa was still watching us with his big, blinkless eyes. So creepy.

Once we were inside the warm and festively decorated grocery store, Mom relaxed a little. "That Santa was kind of gross," I said.

Mom shushed me. "Don't be mean, Hannah. He's just trying to be charitable." Mom pulled out a cart and pushed it with us to the far end of the store where Mom handed us the grocery list. "I'm going to the pharmacy. I'm almost out of my insomnia medicine.

You two can get a head start on picking up the items on that list."

I nodded and took the cart. Jack looked at me with big eyes through his big glasses.

"Do you want to push?" I offered.

He smiled. I got out of his way. I read the items while he pushed the cart.

"Okay, we need some onions, eggs, flour..."

"Hey, Hannah?"

"Yeah?"

"I don't like him, either."

"Who?"

"That Santa outside. He was like one of the homeless guys at the train terminal. Getting right up in your face and asking for money. He was like a smelly, homeless vampire Santa."

I laughed and then forced myself to stop, "Okay, that's not nice, Jackie."

We picked out the items on the list. When we got to the dairy aisle to get the milk and eggs, we saw him again. The creepy Santa was next to the cooler. He had the door wide open. His head was back and he was gulping straight from a carton of eggnog. He wasn't being very careful about it, either and it was dripping on his fake beard and red shirt. He finished the whole thing and then turned his head and looked right at us, his tiny pupils like gun sights trained on us. He never seemed to blink.

"Maybe we don't need eggs or milk that bad."

"Yeah, I don't even like eggs and milk," my brother agreed.

We both started backing up slowly when we bumped into someone right behind us. I nearly jumped out of my skin. Jack yelped a little bit too.

"What has gotten into you two?" Mom asked us.

"Um, nothing, just..." I didn't know exactly what to say. I just looked back at the fishy Santa. He was back to chugging eggnog. I looked back at Mom and she saw him, too.

"Okay, I got my medicine," she said, still watching the strange Santa. She was about to say something else and realized she was distracted and came back to us, "Did you guys get all the stuff on the list?"

"Yep," said Jack "Except for milk and eggs."

Santa finished his drink, wiped his mouth, and then walked away. We waited for him to be gone before we grabbed the milk and eggs.

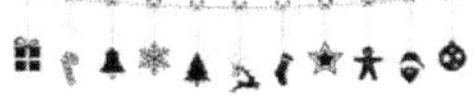

After the groceries were bagged and Mom paid the cashier, we headed back out. Santa was back at his post, ringing his bell again. His back was facing us as he was asking for donations from the people entering. Mom tried to take a wide turn, hoping to avoid Santa's attention, but just as we were passing him his bell stopped ringing.

"You have the money for the children?"

"Oh. Shoot. I forgot," said Mom. I wasn't sure if she meant it or not.

"But you promised," Santa reminded her. His eyes were big and strange—wet-looking.

"Well. I'll get you next time." She started pushing the cart again, but Santa stood in front, blocking her path.

"When?"

"What?"

"When will you be here again?"

"I, uh, I don't know. Please, we're in a hurry." Mom started gesturing to us to stand behind her so she was between us and Santa.

"Your children get everything they want. But I'm raising money for children who don't."

"Ok, thanks," and Mom motioned for us to follow her. We did. As we walked through the parking lot as fast as we could without running, I realized Jack was squeezing my hand. I didn't even notice when he started. We got to the car and Mom made us get in right away. She put the groceries in the back as quickly as she could, shut the door, and got in.

I noticed the cart. She hadn't put it back. "Mom, the cart—"

The first half of my sentence turned into a pitiful yell before I could finish. I pointed out the rear window. Santa was out there. Mom yelled too. Jack said a curse word.

"You're a liar! Liars get coal for Christmas!" Santa yelled. He leaned over and slammed on the car with both hands.

"This guy is crazy!" yelled Jack.

The parking space in front of ours was empty. Mom gunned it, rocking us back. She went screeching out of the parking space. Mom made a hard turn and we could hear the groceries in the back fall over and start rolling around as the tires squealed. Mom got us out of there as quickly as she could.

When we were back on the road, no one said anything for a little while. Mom kept checking the rearview mirror like she was worried we were being followed by Santa in his sleigh. Finally, she asked us, "Everyone okay?"

We both said yeah.

"Hey, Mom."

"Yeah, what is it honey?"

"You forgot the cart."

"What?"

"You didn't put away the cart."

"It's okay. We were in a hurry."

Jack added, "You never leave the cart. You always put it back."

Mom looked back at him through the rearview mirror

and changed the subject, "And where did you learn that word, Jackie?"

"Uh. I don't know. Which word do you mean?"

"You know which word I mean."

Jack shrugged.

"Don't let me catch you using that kind of language again. Your father will be home in a couple days and he won't like to hear those words."

"Okay," said Jack, and he slouched into his seat like he wanted to make himself smaller. He muttered something under his breath.

"What was that?" Mom asked in that harsh mom voice that all moms use when they're serious.

"I said, I told you guys that Santa was creepy."

Chapter 2

We live in an old farmhouse in the country. We had just moved in a couple of weeks ago and it still felt weird. It used to be Grandpa's before he died. It didn't feel like our home yet. It felt like Grandpa's house but with our stuff inside. Mom loved the house, especially since she has her own office now. She works from home on her computer and she doesn't need to work at the kitchen table anymore. She was home all day but she was always busy in her office. She was there but she wasn't there.

When we pulled up our driveway, there was a beat-up white car already there. The engine was running because I could see the smoke coming out of the tail-pipe.

"Who's that?" I asked.

"I don't know," said Mom. We came to a stop and she told us to wait in the car.

She got out and shut the door behind her. She walked up to the white car and knocked on the window. Then she looked surprised. She took a step back Then she leaned in close like she wasn't sure she could believe what she saw. The door opened up and a handsome man stepped out, just a little younger than Mom. He was dressed casually in jeans and a winter coat. He spread his arms out. Mom waited a moment then finally she walked up to him and hugged him.

"Who the heck is that?" Jack asked me.

"I don't have any idea."

The man was hugging her longer than she hugged back and finally, she got him to stop by tapping the man on the back. He had a big smile on his face. She didn't.

I opened my door. "No! Mom said stay in the car!" I ignored Jack and took one step out of the door, stood up and called out to her.

"Is everything okay?"

The man turned to me and his smile got even bigger when he saw me.

"Oh my gosh! Hannah?"

"Uh. Yeah?"

"You are so big now! Holy smokes!" He started walking to our car. Mom had her arms folded and watched us.

"Mom?" I asked.

"It's fine. This is your uncle Charles."

"We have an Uncle Charles?" Jack asked.

Uncle Charles came up to me and gave me a big bear hug. "I cannot believe how grown up you are. I've missed so much since I've been gone. How old are you now? ten?"

"I'm twelve."

"Where have you been?" Jack asked.

Charles let me go and he leaned into the window to get a look at Jack. "That you, Killer?"

"Killer?" Jack and I asked at the same time.

"It is! Hey, Jack. I haven't seen you since you were in diapers, little man! If Hannah's twelve, that makes you ten, right?"

"How come we never heard about you?" Jack asked.

"I've been away."

"But where were you?" I asked.

Charles hesitated to answer and forced a smile. He looked at Mom and asked, "Genie?"

She didn't look too happy. She shook her head no.

What was she saying 'no' to?

Charles looked back at us, "I've been away. In Alaska."

"Oh."

"Charles just stopped by for a minute, kids. Come on out and help with the groceries."

Charles and Mom stepped out of earshot and started a conversation. Charles seemed genuinely happy but Mom didn't. We had to rebag all the groceries because they spilled out of the bags during our escape. 'Killer' and I grabbed as much as we could and went inside, setting the bags on the kitchen table. I could see out the window over the sink that Mom and Uncle Charles were still talking. She was crying a little. What's going on? Finally, they hugged again and when they were done, Mom was smiling.

Uncle Charles saw me looking at them. He started waving me back outside. I grabbed Jack and we went back into the cold to see what our newly-discovered uncle wanted.

"You have more to bring in," said Uncle Charles.

"No, we got it all in one trip," said Jack

"Not all of it." He popped the trunk of his car. Jack and

I walked around to see the trunk was packed full of wrapped Christmas presents and a whole lot more groceries.

"What?" Jack said loudly.

"You still have to carry in all the Christmas presents I brought!"

"Alright!" Jack started filling his arms with as many brightly colored boxes as he could. I looked at Mom. She was wiping her tears and she sniffled but she was smiling. It wasn't a fake smile, either. It was so strange how quickly Mom went from upset to happy. I took some packages and so did Mom and Uncle Charles and we went inside.

Once all the presents were under the tree and all the groceries were put away, Mom and Uncle Charles talked about memories they shared when they used to live in this house when they were kids. Mom was really happy. Charles brought cider and mulling spices and he showed Jack and I how to warm them up on the stove. It filled the house with smells of apple, cinnamon and cloves. It was strange. It started feeling like Christmas as soon as he was in the house.

"What a strange day, huh?" Mom asked.

"How so?" asked Charles.

"Well first there was Vampire Santa at the store and then you showed up unexpectedly."

"Vampire Santa?"

Jack explained the whole event from start to finish, without skipping any details.

"Wow, what a nutcase! He sounds dangerous."

Mom said it wasn't as bad as Jack made it sound. She was always doing that. She always tried to make things sound better than they were. Charles insisted that he would call the grocery store or the charity and complain but Mom insisted he shouldn't. Vampire Santa would be gone after Christmas anyway.

Charles brought a ton of food for dinner and he cooked us a feast. He made a big pot roast, an apple pie, and mashed potatoes.

We sat down to eat but before Jack could start stuffing his face, Uncle Charles held out his hands. Jack stopped with his fork-full of potatoes halfway between his plate and his open mouth. Mom took one of Charle's hands. She reached out to Jack. He took hers. Charles took my left hand and I took Jack's with my right. Uncle Charles bowed his head and started reciting a prayer, thanking the Lord for the meal and thanking him for the gift of family, and finally after he said, "Amen," Jack got back to eating as fast as he could.

"We don't normally pray at dinner, Charles," Mom said.

"Oh, I'm sorry. I shouldn't have presumed to "

"No, no, It's fine, it's fine. It was nice, actually."

Charles continued, "I rediscovered my spiritual side while I was in Corr—Alaska."

"Corr—Alaska?" asked Jack with a mouth full of food.

Mom reminded him not to speak with a mouth full and Uncle Charles continued, "I meant to say Anchorage. I fumbled my words."

"What did you do there? Are you a chef?" I asked. I meant to say it as a compliment because his food was unbelievable.

"Yes, in fact."

"Really?"

"I can totally tell," added Jack.

"Well, a cook. Not a chef, really. What do you kids do?"

"What do you mean? We're kids. We don't have jobs."

Charles and Mom laughed and Charles clarified, "No, what do you do for fun? What do you guys like?"

Mom took the opportunity to brag about us and answered, "Well, Hannah is a very gifted athlete. She carried her team to the nationals last year in softball."

"I'm not on that team anymore," I reminded her, "We moved."

Mom gave me a look that said, "Don't start with me right now," without saying a word.

"That's very impressive, Hannah. I'm sure you'll take this team all the way when the next season starts."

"We'll see," I said.

"You know, your mom was a real athlete, too."

"What? No way!"

"Oh come on," Mom started to try to stop him but he went on.

"She got into college with a gymnastics scholarship."

Jack snorted, "What? Mom was a gymnast?"

"How come you never told us?"

"It was nothing." Mom waved it away.

"No, it wasn't nothing, Genie. You were really good. They don't give scholarships out to women who aren't good."

Mom was looking a little embarrassed and changed the subject, "And Jack is a very strong student. He skipped a grade."

"Wow, Killer! Nice one!"

Jack and I looked at each other silently just mouthing the word, "Killer?"

"Jack is very good at science. He's working on a big project right now for the science fair."

"What are you working on?"

"It's an all-natural cleaning solution. It's made of lemon juice, salt, and some vegetable extracts."

"Very cool," said Uncle Charles, "Can I see?"

"Yeah!"

Mom started saying, "After dinner," but Jack was too quick.

Jack shot up and raced toward the stairs. Uncle Charles got up and followed him, then so did Mom and I. When we got upstairs to Jack's room, my brother was already showing off his spray and the tri-fold display that showed the chemistry of why it works.

"That's really something," said Charles, "Hey, Hannah, can I see your room?"

"I don't have anything interesting in there."

"Yes you do," Mom corrected. "Come on, I'll show you." She led us to my room.

"Whoa!" said Charles, "That is a lot of trophies!"

I shrugged. I had a few but it was no big deal. Charles leaned in and looked at them closely and started reading them out loud, "You have like six trophies for softball tournaments!"

I corrected him, "Eight, actually." I realized I was smiling and I tried to force it back. I didn't want to seem proud.

"And you have trophies for volleyball and kayaking? I didn't even know they give out trophies for kayaking."

"It's no big deal."

After dinner, Charles served us the apple pie. He and Mom stayed up late talking about stuff while Jackie worked on his homework I was on my phone reaching out to my friends from our old town. When we first moved, I heard back from them instantly. But now it felt like it was taking longer and longer to hear back and the messages they sent me were getting shorter and shorter. I missed our old town. I missed my friends. The house was nice but I didn't know anyone at school yet. Jack was doing just fine. He never needed lots of friends. Most of his friends were strangers he met online playing video games.

Mom knocked on my door while I was at my desk I took out my headphones.

"Yeah?"

"Charles is going to stay with us for a few days. So he'll be sleeping on the fold-out couch in the living room. And it's a school night, so don't stay up too late."

"Okay."

"Okay," Mom was about to leave, then asked, "Are you?"

"Am I what?"

"Are you okay?"

"Yeah. I'm fine." I wasn't. But it felt good to see that she noticed and asked.

"Okay." I could tell she didn't believe me, but she left me alone.

Chapter 3

I woke up in my bed, in the light blue glow of the computer screen on my desk.

I looked at the time and it was just past midnight. I groaned, rolled onto my stomach and put my pillow over my head. Then I thought I heard something. I took the pillow off and sat up. I heard it again. A bell ringing. I looked at my computer to see if I left a movie on. No, it wasn't the computer. I heard it again, a high-pitched jingle. Where is it coming from? I rubbed my eyes and climbed out of bed. Jingle-jangle! I looked out the window but my mind was still fuzzy from waking up. I heard it again but I couldn't see anything. It was coming from outside. Maybe someone's cow got loose and was wandering in our yard.

The security lights popped on. They flood the yard with bright lights anytime there is any movement outside. Usually, it's just deer or raccoons in the yard. Just on the edge of the light, I saw something. I gasped and my hands went to my mouth. My blood went cold. Was that someone out there? They were far away and I could just barely see them. The lights went out again. Then I heard it. That jingle. That same jingle from the donation Santa at the grocery store. I froze. Is that him out there? Should I go tell Mom? Then the lights clicked on again. I squinted so I could see as sharply as possible. Then I saw something move. A deer. I exhaled deeply. I didn't realize I'd been holding my breath. I felt my body relax.

"Okay. It's no big deal, Hannah," I told myself out loud. "It's just a deer."

I climbed back into bed. And just as I felt myself dozing off, I heard it again. That bell. Where is it coming from? I didn't sleep well that night.

My alarm clock woke me up. My first thought was, wondering if I had just dreamed about the bell. My second thought was that today was the last day before Winter Break. I got up and went to the bathroom to take a shower. I always take a shower before school. I like my showers hot; so hot they fog up the room. I was tired. I barely got any sleep the night before. Was I imagining that bell? What was that?

I got out of the shower and started toweling myself off. I was about to wipe the fog off the mirror; that's when I saw it.

"What?" I asked no one.

Written on the foggy mirror were the words, Ho, ho, ho.

I swallowed hard. I was spooked at first, I'll admit it. But then I got angry. I dried off, brushed my teeth, got dressed, and stormed downstairs to the kitchen. Jack was already there, taking a Pop-Tart out of the toaster and spreading butter on it—one of his weird habits.

"Very funny, Killer!" I said.

Jack sat down and started reading something on his tablet and eating his buttery Pop-Tart without looking at me.

"What's funny?"

"You know what!"

"Not really," he said, still not looking at me.

"The bell? Ho ho ho? It's all very funny. You got me. But you better watch out because I'll get you back!"

"I don't know what you're talking about."

"Whatever. I'm not even going to tell Mom about this, so you're lucky."

I was seething and didn't want to speak with him. Finally, he broke the silence, looked up from his tablet, and asked, "Why is everyone calling me Killer now?"

Charles packed our lunches before we left the house—leftover roast beef sandwiches, and he handed them to us on the way out. It was an ordinary bus ride and an ordinary day at school. Most of the kids were talking about the vacations they had planned. They didn't tell me about it. I just overheard the other kids talking.

At lunchtime, the kids filled the cafeteria. I still didn't know exactly where to sit. Everyone already had seats. I picked a spot at a table where there weren't a lot of kids already. I hadn't even started my lunch yet when Jack showed up at my table, standing over me.

"I don't even want to talk to you right now," I said.

"Not cool, Hannah."

"After your little pranks, I don't care what you think is cool."

"I don't know what you think I did but I did not deserve this!"

"Deserve what?"

Jack opened up his lunch bag and emptied it on the table. It was just some coal. "You don't mess with a man's lunch, Hannah! Too far!"

"I didn't do that!" I was a little offended by the accusation.

I opened up my lunch bag and looked inside. I emptied it on the table. I had coal, too.

"What's going on, Hannah?" Jack asked me.

"I don't know. I thought it was you!"

"I'm not a prank guy! Phil is the prank guy!"

"Who's Phil?"

Jack pointed to the table he was sitting at. A heavy-set kid wearing a t-shirt with art from a Japanese cartoon waved back. Great. Jack was already making friends faster than I was.

"Well, did Phil do this?"

"No way! Phil's pranks are way more sophisticated!"

"Whatever. It wasn't you and it wasn't me. Who was it ringing the bell?"

"What bell?" Jack asked.

I explained everything and Jack swore to me he didn't do any of it and I believed him. Finally, Phil called out to him, "Hey, Killer! Come see this video! It's hilarious." He was pointing to his phone.

"Killer?" I asked.

"I told the guys at that table that's what Uncle Charles calls me. Now they call me that too."

Jack has two friends already, and a cool nickname. Just lovely. As I was busy pitying myself I noticed we were being watched. Not by any of the kids. The janitor. He was looking across the lunchroom. I looked behind me. There was nothing there but a wall with some nutrition posters on it. I looked back at the janitor. Was he looking at me and Jack? His face was thin and gaunt. He stared for a moment that felt like a hundred moments and he didn't blink. Where had I seen him before? Then he suddenly went back to work, pushing his mop and bucket.

What's that guy's issue?

Chapter 4

"Hannah, where's your head at?"

"What?"

The gym teacher, Ms. Jeffreys was talking to me, her voice echoed in the gymnasium loud enough that it boomed over the sounds of squeaking sneakers on the hardwood floor and the girls yelling, "I'm open!" She had the physique of a polar bear in short gym shorts, a t-shirt, and knee-high socks under tennis shoes.

"What's the problem? You don't like sports?"

The basketball game in progress stopped. The other girls stopped worrying about scoring points and started watching me and Ms. Jeffreys.

"No, I do. I'm good at sports."

"It sure doesn't seem that way." She put her hands on her hips.

"I didn't get any sleep last night. I'm having trouble concentrating. I spaced out."

"Well tonight, how about you get to sleep at a reasonable hour instead of texting with your boyfriend all night. How's that sound?"

A couple of the other girls snickered and tried to cover their mouths with their hands to stop themselves and their laughs came out as snorts.

"I wasn't talking to my boyfriend."

"I don't care about your love life, Hannah," and Ms. Jeffreys blew her whistle.

The girls resumed the game. I tried saying, "No, I mean I don't have a boyfriend," but no one cared and they went back to playing basketball.

After gym class, I had to get back into my regular school clothes. I always change inside the bathroom stalls because I don't like changing in front of others. I had just gotten dressed when I heard it. The bell. The same bell. That jingle-jangle I heard the previous night. My heart felt like it stopped. I stepped onto the toilet and peeked out over the stall. Other girls were changing and didn't seem to notice anything was wrong.

"Hey," I asked, "Anyone else hear that?" The other girls quieted down.

"Hear what?" one girl asked.

"That ringing?"

"No."

Then it rang again. A different girl said, "Yeah, I heard it that time."

"Where is it coming from?" I asked.

The same girl pointed to my locker, "Inside there." The girls went back to chatting as usual. I stepped down from the toilet and opened the bathroom stall door. I walked toward my locker slowly. The rest of the girls were finishing up changing and leaving to go to their next class. I approached my locker, swallowed hard and reached for the door.

"Gah!" was the noise I made when I jumped out of my skin. The bell rang again. It was definitely inside my locker. My heart was beating so hard I could feel my pulse inside my neck I looked around me. I saw someone had left a water bottle. I took the bottle and wrapped it in a towel, and tied it up so it had a handle. I swung it around to make sure it would work It did. I had a makeshift flail. I started swinging it in a circle, ready to smash whoever was hiding in the locker. I reached with my left hand and unlatched it.

I swung the door open and did my best attempt at a

battle cry swinging the water bottle into the locker. It only hit my backpack. I exhaled a deep breath. Where was the jingle coming from?

I heard it again and saw the screen on my phone light up. I picked it up and looked. Someone had sent me some texts. The jingle was coming from the phone. Someone had changed the ringer on it.

Then I felt a big hand on my shoulder and panicked, and swung around. I almost clobbered Ms. Jeffreys in the face with my bottle!

"Whoa! Hannah!"

"Oh my gosh, I'm so sorry, I didn't realize it was you!"

"That's okay but I don't think you were gonna hurt me too bad with just a towel."

She didn't realize I had a heavy, metal bottle full of water inside it.

She went on, "You have to make your next class. Hurry it up. The janitor needs all the girls out of here before he can clean this place before the break."

I grabbed my stuff and left as quickly as I could. On the way out, I saw the janitor waiting by the door, wearing his gray jumpsuit and baseball hat. The same guy from the lunchroom. Up close, his face looked withered like tree bark, and he had great wide eyes and tiny pupils. He was busy picking sardines out of a can and dangling the wet fish into his mouth before dropping them in. It was disgusting.

I rushed past him and headed for my next class. As I was walking away, I heard him say, "You and your brother have a good Christmas."

I turned and said, "Thanks, you too," out of habit, but he wasn't there. He must've gone in to clean, I guess.

The day was pretty boring. There were a lot of tests. The only good thing that happened is that a girl named Candace from my gym class complained about losing her water bottle during 5th period. I realized it must be the one I used when I checked my gym locker. I tapped her on the shoulder and gave it to her. She was thankful and she said she owed me one. It was nice.

At the end of the day, I got onto the bus. Jack was already in his usual seat, looking out the window. I sat next to him.

"Hey."

"Hey."

"I don't want to blame you for anything but I have to ask. Did you change the ringer sound on my phone for text messages?"

"Of course not! I don't know your password."

"Okay, I'm sorry. I didn't want to blame you again but I had to ask to rule you out as a suspect." I told him about what happened during gym class.

"Somebody is messing with us really bad! But why?"

I shrugged.

"What were the messages?"

"I totally forgot to look!" I opened up my phone and we leaned in near each other so we could both see. Three texts from the same unregistered phone number. The number had a foreign international area code.

They were just images. The first one was a picture of my diary, opened up to a page where I wrote down all of my passwords. I gasped. The second picture was from outside the house. It was at night. The only light came from my window. I zoomed in on the picture using my thumb and forefinger. It was me! Looking out the window the night before! Someone was out there!

"Hannah, I'm getting really scared."

"Me, too."

"I don't even want to see the third picture."

"We have to."

I opened up the last image. But it wasn't an image. It was a video of a rubber Santa mask. Someone was making its mouth move like a puppet, while it mouthed along with "Here Comes Santa Claus," which was playing in the background. But it was just those words, and it repeated on a loop over and over again. The rubber Santa head looked disfigured and deflated; almost melted. Its mouth flapped along to the song, it's eyes were empty and hollow and black.

"I hate this video so much," said Jack, who was holding himself like he was suddenly very cold.

Chapter 5

The moment the bus dropped us off in front of Grandpa's house—I mean our house, Jack and I ran up the driveway and straight in through the front door, yelling "Mom, Mom!"

Uncle Charles found us first. "What's going on? What's wrong?"

"Where's Mom, we need to tell her something!"

"She's upstairs working."

We ran up the stairs and into Mom's office; she was surprised to see us. Jack and I both started telling her everything that had happened as fast as we could at the same time.

Mom was not able to follow what we were saying. She told us to take a breath and explain one at a time. We did. She seemed skeptical. First we showed her the coal. And then we showed her the text messages. She immediately called the police. When the police promised her they were sending over an officer to take a statement, Mom grabbed both of us and squeezed us as hard as she could.

A police officer came and knocked on the door. Charles let her in. When she saw our uncle, she seemed surprised.

"Charles."

"Hi, Miriam."

"It's been a while."

"Sure has."

"Staying out of trouble?"

"Always."

"Mm hm." She turned her attention to Mom, me, and Jack. She introduced herself as Officer Miriam Pinsky and she asked what she could do for us. Mom gave her a place to sit on the couch. Charles went to the kitchen to make coffee.

We told her our story. She seemed concerned, too, which was a relief. It seemed so crazy it was hard to believe. She asked us a lot of questions and we didn't have good answers to most of them. We didn't know much. I was glad that people believed us. She wrote everything down on a notepad. One question she asked over and over was, "Do you know anyone who would wish you harm?" But we didn't know.

Finally, I had a thought. "Wait, but maybe. No. That's not right."

"No, go ahead," said the policewoman.

"Could it be... Vampire Santa?"

"Who?" The officer was confused.

Mom told her the whole story and Officer Pinsky took down as many notes as she could.

"Ny-Ålesund." Uncle Charles appeared from seemingly out of nowhere carrying a tray with coffee on it. He set the tray on the coffee table and took a seat in Dad's chair.

"What's that mean?" asked Officer Pinsky.

"I just looked up the area code for that phone number that was harassing Hannah. That's the name of the city it came from."

"That's strange."

"It's the northernmost town in the world."

"How do you know that?" asked the officer.

"I just looked it up." Charles held up his phone to show he had just searched about it online.

"So that means it's the town closest to..." Jack started.

"...the North Pole," I finished his thought.

Officer Pinsky stood up and promised us that she would look into whoever this Vampire Santa guy from the grocery store was. She told us we should leave the house in the meantime.

"He knows where you live and has already been inside the house. Do you have any friends or relatives you can stay with?"

We said no.

You should try and find a hotel to stay at until we can figure this out."

Mom was a little iffy, but Uncle Charles insisted we should. Finally, she agreed.

We saw the officer out and Mom told us to start packing. Jack went upstairs. I was about to but then I got curious.

"Hey, Uncle Charles?"

"What's up, Hannah?"

"How do you know Officer Pinksy?"

"We went to high school together."

"Oh. Why did she ask if you were staying out of trouble?"

Uncle Charles laughed, "Well, I used to be kind of a trouble-maker when I was a kid."

"What kind of trouble?"

"Don't worry about it, kiddo. It was just dumb kid stuff. Do you need any help packing?"

"No, I'm fine."

I went upstairs and on my way to my room I saw Jack sniffing his clothes.

"What are you doing, weirdo?" I half laughed.

"Smell this." Jack held up a pair of his pants.

I laughed, "No way!"

Jack's shoulders went limp and his chin went up like he was exhausted by my laughter, "Come on, Hannah! The clothes are clean, they just... I don't know. Come here and smell it."

I came in and hesitantly, very cautiously gave a tiny but distant sniff.

"This reeks of peppermint."

"Doesn't it? That's weird right?"

"I don't get it."

"Me neither."

"You think someone put peppermint all over your clothes?"

Jack shrugged. He started taking more clothes out of his dresser and then he fell back onto his butt on the floor and yelped. "What the heck!"

I looked into the drawer. His socks were all stuffed with little items, just like stockings over the fireplace. I cautiously picked one up and looked inside. These weren't ordinary stocking stuffers. Inside one of the socks were rusty nails, a pair of gross old dentures, the head of a stuffed reindeer toy, a couple of corroded batteries, and a hypodermic needle. I dropped the sock as soon as I saw that. I knew better than to mess with needles. I called for Mom and she came right up.

Mom and Charles did a thorough search of our rooms to make sure there weren't any more surprises. All of Jack's socks were stuffed. Mom put on some gardening gloves to protect her hands from the sharp things in the sock and put all the socks into a rubber bin in case the police needed it as evidence.

I heard Mom and Uncle Charles talking in Mom's office. I couldn't make out what they were saying but it sounded serious so I walked over there quietly, hoping to hear. They were whispering so I peeked in. Mom saw me right away and quickly stood in front of her computer monitor so I couldn't see what was on it. But I did see it, just for a second. Her email was open and someone had sent her pictures of dead reindeer—hunted probably. Mom reached behind her to turn off the screen, like I wouldn't know. That was Mom. Trying to pretend the bad stuff isn't that bad.

"What is it, hun?"

"Um, nothing. I just... We usually have a snack after school and we're hungry."

"I totally forgot! I'm sorry, honey," said Mom.

"I'll make something," said Charles.

"Nothing with peppermint, please," I added.

Chapter 6

We didn't know how long we'd need to be gone for so we stuffed as much as we could into our duffle bags. Mom was busy calling every hotel within 50 miles but they seemed to be all booked up for Christmas. She paced up and down the hall, clearly getting frustrated. She was put on hold and had to hang up to take an incoming call.

"Yes? Yes. Okay. Uh huh. Gerald Forrester? No, I don't think I know who that is."

I walked toward Mom to hear her half of the conversation.

"You're kidding! I can't believe that! That's... I just... I'm speechless. Well I'm glad! I will definitely be bringing this up at the next PTA meeting, I can tell you that much!" Mom's face had a lot of mixed emotions. She seemed happy, angry and confused, all at the same time.

Jack and Uncle Charles came into the house from outside where they were making snowmen. "What's going on?"

Mom held up a hand to shush her brother long enough to finish her conversation. "Yes. Yes. That's great. Thank you so much. Thank you. You too. Goodbye." She hung up and tossed her phone onto the couch. She put her hands on her hips, and looked at us.

"Unbelievable!"

"What?" asked Charles.

"You know that Santa who was bothering us at the grocery store the other day?"

"Yeah, of course," said Jack.

"He works at your school."

"He does?" Jack and I answered at the same time.

"Mr. Forrester."

"Who's that?" I asked.

"The janitor?" asked Jack.

"The janitor," said Mom.

I could feel the pieces come together in my brain. Those big eyes. That fishy smell. That general weirdness. Of course, it was him! That's why he was creeping around me at school! I looked at Jack and he looked at me. We could see we both were having the same realization.

"Do you know him? Have you kids ever spoken to him?" Mom asked.

Jack shook his head. I didn't want to freak Mom out any more than she already was, so I said, "Uh, no, not really. He said Merry Christmas to me the other day."

"After the grocery store thing?"

"Uh, yeah."

Mom rushed up and hugged me tightly. "Too... hard..." I said. Her other arm got Jack too, and she crushed us with a big bear hug. Finally, she released us. Her eyes were getting watery.

"Listen, someone already complained to the grocery store. He was fired yesterday, so he can't be a Santa there anymore. And I'm about to complain to the school as soon as their office is open. It's not okay for a maniac like that to be near kids."

"So it's been our janitor doing all these things?" asked Jack. He wasn't really asking, he was just trying to make it all make sense.

"Thank God they got that dirtbag. The schools and

charities need to be more careful about who they hire," Uncle Charles added

Mom continued, "The police said they are already at his house, asking him questions. They said they might arrest him if they can. If not, they'll just keep him under surveillance. And Officer Pinsky also promised to keep an officer outside the house in the driveway tonight, just to be extra safe."

"Are we still going to a hotel?" I asked.

"I guess not. We don't really need to anymore."

Uncle Charles jumped in, "Hold on. This Forrester guy isn't under arrest yet, okay. And we don't one hundred percent know it's him, right? Innocent until proven guilty? So I think we should all just play it safe and get a hotel tonight."

"They're going to have a person at his house watching him and they'll have an officer right outside. And I've been looking for a hotel for almost two hours. There's nothing."

"Don't minimize this, Genie. You do that. You try to pretend bad things aren't as bad as they are." Charles was right about that, to be honest.

That got Mom mad. She didn't get mad often. When

she did, she didn't raise her voice or move around a lot. She did the opposite. She'd talk real quietly and her body would become rigid. It's a lot scarier her way, believe me. "That's really rich coming from you, Charles. It really is."

Charles backed off. He clapped his hands together and put on a big smile and said, "Okay! We're staying in tonight! Cozy family time at home. How about we play Clue and have ice cream after dinner?"

After a delicious dinner, our chef uncle showed us the dessert he'd prepared. He came out with a tray with bowls of ice cream. "Ta-da!"

"Oh! What is it?" asked Jack.

"A Christmas-themed, homemade eggnog ice cream, with crumbles of gingerbread mixed in!"

"Oh wow! That looks lovely! Thank you!" Mom took a bowl and started enjoying it.

Charles held the tray in front of Jack but he made a face and said, "No thank you."

"What? Why not?"

"I'm allergic to ginger."

"What? I didn't even know that was possible."

"Yeah, I get all rashy and I get bad diarrhea."

"Okay, well then there's more for Hannah," and Charles brought the tray to me.

I'm sorry."

"What? You too?"

"I don't like gingerbread. Or eggnog."

"You used to love gingerbread! And eggnog!" He looked hurt.

"Maybe when I was like, four years old. I'm sorry, I just... It's kind of gross."

Mom chimed in, "It's fine, I'll eat all of it!"

"Just try it! Come on! Tastes change, maybe you'll like it!"

Mom kept saying it was so good and looking at me to encourage me to try. I took the bowl and tasted a little and I made a face. I wasn't trying to, it just happened. "It's not bad." I was trying to be polite but my face gave me away.

"First Killer, then Hannah. This is mutiny. Okay, well, is

there something else I can make you instead? Brownies or something?" Charles looked a little frustrated.

"I'm good," said Jack. I agreed.

"No dessert?"

"I'm pretty full. I think I'm just going to go to bed," I said.

Jack was already starting to yawn. It had been a long day for both of us. We went upstairs and got ready for bed. I slipped my nightgown over my head before tucking myself in. Maybe nightgowns seem nerdy to you, but they are comfortable and no one from school will ever know.

I opened up my laptop and looked for something to watch. I like to watch TV before bed, sometimes. Everything was Christmas shows. I closed the window to the video streaming website. Some music then. I went to my favorite music streaming site, but it was just Christmas music. All the banners and colors were Christmasified. I sighed and closed that, too. Christmas wasn't for a few more days and I was already sick of it after everything that had happened. I reached out and texted one of my old friends from where we used to live. She didn't get back to me.

I laid flat on my back and reflected on the short time we'd lived here. First impressions are the most important and this town was not winning me over.

Somehow, I didn't feel much better than I did that morning. At some point I dozed off.

Chapter 7

I woke up to the sounds of loud music. I stepped out of bed and the song was playing so loudly I could feel the vibrations in the floor. It was Christmas music. I tried flicking on a light switch but it didn't work.

I peeked out into the hall. Jack was out there in his pajamas, rubbing his eyes with one hand and holding his glasses with the other.

"What's going on?" Jack almost had to yell so I could hear him over the music.

"I don't know," I said. I walked toward Mom's room. I knocked but the music was so loud, she wouldn't hear, so I just walked in. She was sound asleep. How could she sleep through this? I started shaking her and saying her name, but she just muttered something, and shifted a little, and started snoring louder. I shook her harder. She opened her eyes a little and said something like, "I'm never at the coffee shop." Then she closed her eyes again. She must be dreaming. Why wouldn't she get up?

I went back into the hall. Jack was looking over the

banister to the first floor. The house was completely dark except for a flickering, orange glow of light coming from the living room. I yelled down, "Uncle Charles? Is that you?" as loud as I could. I told Jack to stay upstairs as I walked down the stairs slowly and cautiously. Downstairs a song was playing:

On the night before Christmas when Santa is near

All the children to dreamland will soon disappear

But there's one little darling who won't close an eye

Till you call for the sandman with this lullaby

At the bottom of the stairs, I looked around. I sniffed a couple of times.

"Is that gingerbread?" Something touched my back I jumped, startled, and spun around. "Jack, I said stay upstairs!"

He grabbed my nightshirt. "I don't want to be up there alone!"

"Fine, but stay close, okay?"

He nodded.

We walked slowly into the warm living room. Charles must have started a fire in the fireplace. We peeked over the backside of the couch. "Charles?" He wasn't sitting there. We came around to the front of it. Charles wasn't lying there either, instead there was a big red stain where he usually slept.

"Oh no! Is that? Is that blood?"

Jack repeated the curse word that Mom told him to never say. I grabbed Jack by the arm and ran to the front door, threw it open, and ran outside barefoot, into the snow. It must have been zero degrees out. It was so cold. I started calling out to the officer. The security lights clicked on. The police car was gone.

"Where... where did the police go?"

"They were supposed to be out here protecting us!"

I looked around in both directions. It was pitch black out. The clouds covered up the moon. We were deep in the country and the nearest neighbor would take fifteen minutes to walk to. I could hear Jack's teeth chattering. My feet were already feeling pins and needles and we'd only been outside for a minute.

"Back inside!" I said.

"But—"

"We'll freeze out here! We need to get our boots and coats!"

We ran back to the house. When we got there, the door was locked.

"Why did you lock the door?" yelled Jack

"I didn't! Or maybe I did by accident! Come on!"

I took him by the hand and ran around to the back of the house. The backyard was full of snowmen blocking the back door. There must have been 15 of them, at least! But they were strange. They were misshapen. They had asymmetrical faces, agonized, drooping mouths and sad eyes. They looked like they were in pain.

"What is going on?" Jack asked me. Of course, I didn't know any better than he did.

The horrific snowmen were all close together, no more than a couple feet between them. I led and Jack followed. We walked slowly, carefully between the snowmen as they looked at us like they were crying for help. We didn't want to disturb them. Who knows who or what was inside.

"I hate these snowmen, Hannah," Jack whispered.

"Me too, Killer."

We got past them and made it to the back door. I pressed the code on the keypad and it unlocked. We heard a thump behind us and we both yelled. We turned but no one was there. Just the snowmen, with one of them now headless. We must have bumped it by accident.

We hurried inside and shut the door. We were in the kitchen. Someone had done some redecorating. All over the kitchen, on every surface, someone had spray-painted the words "Ho ho ho," over and over again in red paint. It was on the walls, the ceiling, the floor, the refrigerator, the counter, and the oven.

It was nearly dark except for a couple of lit candles. Jack was blowing hot breath into his hands to get warm. We walked through and could see the oven was on. It smelled like gingerbread cookies.

"I don't want to look in there!"

"Me neither," I agreed. I picked up one of the candles to help us see in the dark

We walked past the oven, out of the kitchen into the foyer, and opened up the closet. But our coats and shoes were missing.

I sniffed. Something was burning. We walked back into the living room. Our coats and boots were in the fire!

"Now what?"

"We need to call the police!"

"My phone's upstairs."

"Mine too."

We both ran up the stairs as fast as we could. I went into my room, Jack went into his. I know I left it next to my bed but it wasn't there. I ripped the blanket and pillow off my bed and threw them across the room. I pushed things out of the way. It wasn't there. I went back out into the hall. Jack came out too.

"My phone's gone!" said Jack.

"Mine too."

Suddenly, the music cut out. It was just perfect silence except for the distant crackle of our winter clothes and a log in the fireplace.

Jingle-jangle. Jingle-jangle. That bell. It was coming from downstairs.

I walked cautiously to the banister and looked over. At the foot of the stairs, blocking the path to the front door, was a grim Santa Claus. This wasn't the jolly Christmas elf from TV. This person was wearing a terrifying, rubber Santa mask. The same mask from the video someone sent me. It was twisted in a caricature of a smile. You couldn't see his eyes, though. Just two black pits like the holes in a skull, its mouth partially open, like he was saying "Ho ho ho," but it made no sound.

Jack started screaming. I felt like I should be screaming, too, but no sound came out of my mouth. Jack grabbed me hard and half hid behind me.

Rubberface Santa held up a couple of cell phones so we could see. Our cell phones. He put them in his pocket. He reached behind him and when I could see his hand again he was holding a big pointy hook. It was big as a crowbar, and it was painted with twisting red and white stripes like a candy cane.

That's when I started screaming too.

Chapter 8

We ran into my room. I slammed the door shut and locked it.

I started pushing my dresser in front of the door. "Help me!" I yelled. I took Jack's hand and stepped back. We stood there and just stared at the door. It couldn't have been more than a few seconds but it felt like time slowed down to a crawl as we just waited. BAM! BAM! BAM! We literally jumped. Santa was hammering on the door. Jack started crying. Then we heard scraping. The scraping of a hook on the other side of the door.

I opened up my closet and found my aluminum bat. I raised it like I would knock his head into the bleachers if he got in. I waited but the scratching stopped and the loud music came back on.

Here comes Santa Claus, here comes Santa Claus

Right down Santa Claus lane

Vixen and Blitzen and all his reindeer

Pullin' on the reins

"We can't stay here," I said.

Bells are ringin', children singin'

All is merry and bright

"We can't go out there!" said Jack.

So jump in bed and cover your head

'Cause Santa Claus comes tonight!

I opened my closet. "Here, put on some warm clothes."

"These are too big. And they're girl clothes."

"Not now, Jack! Just do it!"

We didn't have jackets or boots so we put on as many layers as we could, several socks on top of each other—anything we could find. We both looked ridiculous but at least we would be warm. I opened the window. "Come on."

I stepped out of the window onto the awning that covers the front porch. It was fiercely cold, the wind was sharp and it stole the heat out of my face. I reached a hand out for Jack. He took it.

"Be careful. It's icy up here."

Jack nodded. I started leading him across the awning

to the only other adjoining window—Jack's room. I peeked inside. It looked empty. I started opening the window as slowly and quietly as I could, but this is an old house and it took some muscle to get it to move at all. I didn't want to force it because it could make a noise. The awning was at an angle and it was a little slippery so it was really tough to force it. So tough that I overdid it a little and slipped. I caught myself but my knees slipped out from under me and I fell onto my belly with a loud thump.

Then I saw a figure move past the door. Oh no! He heard me! I pulled back away from the window and guided Jack to hide from the window, too. Could he see me? No, it's dark outside. I waited a moment. Then I carefully checked again. No one was there. "Okay," I whispered. I finally got the window unstuck, opened it, and I crawled back into Jack's room. Jack followed.

I kept my bat raised high, just in case. "I think we're clear," I whispered.

The man in the Santa mask filled the doorway. Jack and I both screamed in surprise. He took a step into the room. Jack leaped in front of me and started spraying the masked man with a spray bottle.

Rubber face Santa grabbed his face and started yelling, "Ow! My eyes!"

"That's concentrated citric acid and sodium!" Jack yelled.

I wound up and let my bat fly like the bases were loaded. My bat hit his hand that was over his face. He dropped his hook and fell over, "Son of a—"

We stepped out into the hall. Jack kept spraying him and I kept hitting him. He flailed around and he grabbed my bat and yanked it away from me.

I grabbed my brother by his pink sweatshirt and we ran to Mom's room and shut the door. Then we heard some slamming on the door, and yelling, "You brats! You're making this more difficult than it needs to be!"

BAM! BAM! BAM! The door jamb was cracking and splintering. He was going to break down the door any second. Jack hugged onto me tightly. I hugged him back because I didn't know what else to do.

BAM! BAM! BAM!

Then he started singing in a gruff but familiar voice.

"You better watch out..."

BAM!

Jack and I jumped into bed with Mom and started shaking her, "Mom, wake up! Wake up!"

"You better not cry..."

BAM!

Jack covered his ears and closed his eyes tightly.

"You better not pout..."

BAM!

"I'm telling you why..."

BAM!

"Santa Claus..."

BAM!

"is coming..."

BAM!

"to—"

Then it stopped suddenly before he finished the last line. It was quiet for a moment. Then the door unlocked from the outside. How?

The door opened and we saw the silhouette of a large, intimidating figure standing in the doorway. I grabbed the clock from Mom's bedside dresser and I threw it like a pitch in softball and got him right in the head.

"Ow! Hannah! It's me!"

We stopped shouting. Mom woke up a little and said in her sleepy daze, "Oh, is John home? What time is it?" and she fell back asleep.

"Dad?"

"Kids? Are you okay?"

The figure stepped into the room. It was Dad! We jumped up and ran into his arms. He kneeled and scooped us up and gave us a great big hug. He was still in his Army uniform.

"You've really been keeping that arm strong in the off-season, kiddo. Nice throw."

I laughed and my eyes got a little wet.

"What's going on here?" he asked.

Dad let us go. I realized then I was crying a little, half from being scared, half because Dad was home

"Stay here," said Dad. He walked up to the door. Rubber face Santa was on the ground, unconscious. Dad must have walloped him! Dad crouched and pulled the mask off Santa. Jack and I walked up closer so we could see.

"Charles? What?" Dad looked up at us like we might understand.

Jack and I both said the same thing, "Uncle Charles?"

Dad started calling 911. He looked at us and asked, "What's your uncle doing here dressed like Santa? Why is the house completely trashed? And why is your mom asleep?"

Chapter 9

The police finally came back They arrested Charles. He wouldn't even look at us or talk to us as they took him away.

We went to the police station with the officers. We told them everything. Mom was sobbing; half because she felt guilty because she felt like she failed to protect us, and half happy because we were all safe. Charles was in custody and taken to the hospital to treat the injuries that my Dad, brother and I gave him.

They told us that someone made a fake 911 call nearby to lure our police guard away. It was probably Charles who made that call.

A couple of days later, Officer Pinsky came back to the house. Mom and Dad invited her in. She had a cup of coffee and they all sat down in the living room. The officer asked a few very specific questions.

"When did you open your lunch? Where do you keep your diary? How did Charles know about Mr. Forrester?"

When she was done asking questions, she asked, "Can I look at those gifts that Charles brought?"

"Sure. They're still under the tree."

The officer walked to the tree and started ripping the paper off one of them.

"Does this mean we get to have the present early?" asked Jack.

Mom shushed him.

"You don't want this present," said the officer, and she showed us what was inside.

"It's a toaster?" It wasn't even in one piece. It was a busted toaster. The officer opened another present. It was three old tennis shoes that didn't match.

"What the heck is going on, Officer?"

She didn't answer Dad's question. She asked Mom, "Ma'am, you work from home, yes? Do you have an office? Or a room that would be difficult for him to access?"

Mom nodded and showed her upstairs. We all followed. Officer Pinsky looked around the room for a moment. Then she started knocking on the walls. She moved along them to a different spot, giving a little knock every foot or so. Until finally, the knock sounded different.

"This drywall looks newer than the rest."

"Charles did repairs on that wall a few years ago when our dad was still alive."

Officer Pinsky asked if we chopped our own wood. Dad said yes. She asked him to bring her the axe. He went downstairs and about a minute later he came back with the wood axe. The officer took it and started chopping a hole in the wall.

, "Hey you can't do that!" Dad started objecting.

But just a couple of chops later, Dad understood. When the hole was big enough to look into, we could see what all the fuss was about. The wall was full of cash.

"Mom, why is the wall full of money?" I asked.

"I don't know!"

Officer Pinsky explained everything.

"This money was stolen from a bank by your uncle five years ago. He hid it here and fled to Alaska until things cooled off."

"Whoa, whoa. Mom. He said he was a cook."

"He was a cook. In prison. He cooked there."

"You didn't tell us he was a jail bird!" said Jack.

Officer Pinsky continued, "The other members of his bank robbery crew were caught and they ratted out Charles. He was arrested up in Alaska but there wasn't much evidence except the testimony of his accomplices. And the police couldn't even find the money. So Charles pled down to a lesser charge."

"What does that have to do with all of this?" Dad asked.

"When Charles was released, he came back home to get his money. He brought boxes with fake presents because he needed a way to move all that cash out. The problem was he couldn't get into the wall. It's your office and you work from home. Hannah's room is right next to it. Even if he tried opening the wall while Genie was asleep, Hannah would be close enough to hear."

"But why go through all of this?"

"To get you out of the house. You told him about Vampire Santa and that's when he got the idea. He wanted to scare you out of the house by pretending that Vampire Santa was stalking you. But it was Charles all along. That's how he was able to get inside the house."

"How did he switch our lunches while we were at school?" I asked.

"He didn't. He packed your lunches with coal and told you it was sandwiches. When you got to school, he knew you'd assume someone switched them."

"What about the blood on the couch?"

"Well, it definitely isn't Charles' blood. I bet if we tested it we'd find it came from an animal, probably some meat from the grocery store. He just left that to scare you."

"It's just crazy. The mask and everything," Mom said.

"That wasn't his first plan. He hoped you would be so scared from the texts and the bell that you would go to a hotel and leave the house. Then he could sneak back in and get the money out of the wall. Only, you didn't leave."

Mom shook her head.

The officer went on, "That totally messed up his plan. So he tried using your mom's medicine. He put it in the ice cream. But only your mom ate it."

"That's why she wouldn't wake up!"

"Plan A was to get you to go to a hotel. Plan B was to knock everyone out with ice cream. Your dad was coming home in the morning. He needed one last plan. Plan C was to scare you kids and chase you into a room. While you were hiding, he could get the money, leave, hide the money somewhere else, then come back and pretend to be friendly Uncle Charles. And Mr. Forrester would take all the blame."

"He was always troubled—Charles. But I never thought he would be capable of something like this," Dad said.

Mom started sobbing and Dad held her. She apologized to Jack and I. "I thought he'd changed! I really did! He seemed different. He brought those presents and he prayed with us. I can't... I'm just so upset."

Jack and I jumped in and we had a big family hug.

Officer Pinsky promised us Charles wouldn't be bothering us again. Jack also wondered if we would keep the money. Obviously we couldn't, which disappointed him greatly.

We had a great Christmas that year. Dad was home and Mom was always happier when he was around. We kept throwing logs on the fire. The room was toasty and cozy and we listened to Elvis Christmas music—Dad's favorite.

"Hey, Hannah. Can you grab a couple more logs from the shed?"

I got up and put on my new coat and boots. I had to get new ones after Charles burned my last ones. I went out the back door to the woodshed and grabbed a couple logs. When I turned to go back inside, I stopped in my tracks. Mr. Forrester was there just a few feet from me. Dressed like Santa. I dropped my logs.

"I lost my job at the charity. I lost my job at the school. The whole town thinks I'm a creepy Santa who stalks kids. All because you and your Mom didn't want to give money to poor children."

I didn't know what to say or do. Should I scream? Should I apologize? Should I run? My mouth moved like I was going to say something but nothing came out. I felt paralyzed.

Mr. Forrester reached behind him and took out a big chef's knife from his belt and said, "Bad kids get coal for Christmas."

The End

www.ingramcontent.com/pod-product-compliance
Lightning Source LLC
Chambersburg PA
CBHW072233190626
46809CB00017B/1898

9781970565034